IF SO CARRIED BY THE WIND

By

Seth Kupchick

Copyright

IF SO CARRIED BY THE WIND:

Copyright 2016 – Seth Kupchick

All rights reserved

Table of Contents

1. If so carried by the wind
2. Afterword

"Hobo – trekkers that forever search an empire wilderness of freight and rails. Each seemed a child, like me, on a loose perch Holding to childhood like some termless play." Hart Crane, The Bridge

If so carried by the wind

I should have been an actor. Actors are free to be whoever they want whenever they want as long as they stick to the character they're given. When someone compliments an actor, thanking him for his performance of so and so, the artist in him can smile, look at the audience, and know he's done his job. He has created an illusion, and that's what art is, an illusion of the living world. An actor never has to be himself, but is the accumulation of a style filtered through a character. But a writer, an autobiographer, a poet – a man who opens other people's doors and lets them walk in – must be true to his experiences. He must write about the people of his life, however fictional they may seem, however extraordinary, awful, excitable, knowable, or deep. A writer can't slip into a character made for him by a writer, but must make the character from his life. In his heart he knows the truest best writing isn't art at all, but some amalgamation of fiction and reality stewed together in such a way as to rise above art into heaven.

Life at Hal's started with me waking up in an attic room in Quill's cabin. It was a handmade wooden structure about a mile and a half from Hal's place, up a dirt road called Kiler Canyon. It housed me and Casey (Quill, one of Hal's nine children, was gone for much of the month). Casey would sleep downstairs and I upstairs. I don't know how this arrangement was set up but it remained the whole time I was there. By a kerosene lamp (the cabin had no electricity, only a wood burning stove) I'd read Chinese poetry as the moon came through a triangular window. I was comfortable sleeping there and would wake up early in the morning alive for the day. It was September in Paso Robles, California, 1993, and every day was hot. The sun came over the hill early through the oak trees, and the glass had a blazing orange tone to it. The world was all blazing orange and gray, shadows blanketing the bottom of the hills. My car sat like a toy car on the dead-end road outside the cabin, a white '87 Nissan Sentra.

What was I doing on Peachy Canyon road or Kiler Canyon? I'd made a verbal agreement to help Casey edit his book on his best friend John Stephens, who went by the algebraic variable X. The manuscript was five years in the making but we were working on it one year after the movie *Malcolm X* by Spike Lee and Casey was fond of wearing the movie's X cap that took America by storm in the early '90s. He would wait for me to graduate college in June and immediately thereafter we'd start work on the manuscript. Casey said he chose me because he liked my sense of humor. He also told me that all I'd have to do as an editor was laugh at the parts of *X* I thought were funny.

Easier said than done, however. Casey wasn't writing a series of one liners for a standup comic, but a double portrait of himself and X in the '60s. It was clear from the beginning the book was to be not just hundreds of written pages in the form of a novel but a picture book too, an oral biography of other people's impressions of X, poetry and everything but the kitchen sink. Through June, July and August of '93 it was difficult to make anything of it.

Casey was too depressed over his family break-up to really work on the book, but work was what he needed. Hal said so. Casey said so too when he first greeted me in Paso Robles wearing a white preppy sweater someone had given him from the Goodwill. His old lady, Anne had kicked him out earlier in the year, and he'd just lost all his teeth for dentures (Casey had a psycho photo of X getting all of his teeth pulled out at the dentist too). Casey had several children in their twenties and thirties but hadn't raised them, and now his chance to be a live-in daddy was pulled out from under his feet. His two young children, his young lover, it was all going up in smoke, and he couldn't concentrate on his book. That was my job.

One day in August Casey and I sat in the sand of a jungle gym on the west side of Santa Cruz and saw clearly that our artistic project needed a serious push. In my youthful optimism – Casey was 35 years my senior – I thought we could make a book out of it with three weeks of concentration. Casey was dubious, but he wanted to believe, so we decided to take the book to Hal's farm, which Hal had offered to Casey earlier in the year.

What better place to focus than alone in the country in a cabin built by a genius farmer?

I was not at the farm to write my own book but to help Casey edit his on his dead friend John Stephens, aka X. He'd written a thousand interchangeable pages, but one page of writing never followed the next; somehow Casey stuck a thousand pieces of paper into his typewriter (banger, he called it), and let the thing fly, character fragmenting the hell out of X. There was little dialogue or sustained story to hold it together, but flashes of memory – X here, X there. It was my job to disseminate meaning from the mess. I was to mark the pages that were gold, gold being anything that was a good poem portrait of John Stephens, complete and unto itself, or anything that was funny. The rest I was to trash. I went through a thousand pages of the Swami's notes (the name X gave Casey after Casey came back from India in the early '60s) but we couldn't make a book out of it.

I went to Paso Robles giving the project a concentrated month but why not longer? Jenny's new love, a girl I'd met right before graduating, but also because I wasn't the one writing the book, Casey was, and there were only so many pages I could read. I didn't want to ghost write *X,* because I couldn't fill in the stories he'd only sketched. They weren't my memories we were excavating, they were Casey's, though it would have been beyond brilliant if I could have made up X's story for him. I should've been able to given the talks we had about X, and the writings I'd read. *The*

Vagrant's Handbook was Casey's prized piece and had an anecdote about sleeping in ice plants by the sea and included a chapter called *Doin' the Happy Birthday,* all about how to hustle free drinks in a bar by playing "Happy Birthday" on a jukebox and going with the con. Casey also had a cassette of X called *The Dope Operetta,* a musical masterpiece about a freak musician named Heavy Early, and many photographs too. X had curly black hair and a Groucho Marx mustache but if I wrote about him it would have been my fiction further distilled from the truth, not Casey's one step closer, so I didn't write nor did Casey ask me.

He was very depressed at the time. Casey's 10-year relationship with Anne had blown up fiction-size six months earlier and, if that weren't bad enough, there were two kids between them who Casey loved very much. He was 60 and Anne was in her late twenties and sexy, and it was a miracle he had her. He really thought he'd be gettin' it good from her till he died, so the family man oil-painting, dope-smokin' dude was takin' it real bad. In the middle of nowhere, with nothing but oak trees and grass around us, he'd go days without talking. I don't even think "hello" was said much of the time. He'd be outside in the sun, yellow jackets buzzing around, reading a magazine, sometimes with his dentures out, sometimes with them in. Aside from his dentures, Casey was a very young 60. His chest hair was still black (it was so hot we didn't wear shirts much of the time) and so was his full head of hair. His body was still taut and lean, retaining his gymnast's physique, but he had big bushy eyebrows and eyes that grew large with wonder or slithered like a monkey's.

    Most of the day he didn't work on the book. He'd wake up early, read a magazine, stare into nothing, or ask me to drive him to the air-conditioned bookstore in town. Paso Robles was a mile and a half down Kiler Canyon road, a scraggly, narrow, unpaved, tarred road that snaked unevenly. I felt more like a boatman when I was steering the Nissan, because it wasn't like driving at all. It was like maneuvering a rudder; the goal was to keep the car on the highest ground possible. Casey said he'd driven roads like it before in Mexico, but it was murder on the car and I was uptight about driving it. I didn't want to kill my car and it made a horrible screeching sound every time I pushed on the brakes.

I drove it up and down Kiler Canyon anyway. It was something I was hung up on, it's true, and driving it was my test. If I couldn't give up the car, if I was hung up like my parents, then how could I ever get loose enough to live on my own terms? How could I be a slave to a $6,000 Japanese car?

The house in Peachy Canyon was a time warp, and when you opened the door you entered another world a century away. You ducked your head and walked through a very dark front room where, if you weren't careful, you banged it against a wooden beam. Then you walked through Hal and Martha Chase's bedroom with a bed and a little window facing east to watch the sunrise. From their room you stumbled into the kitchen; they had the only room connected to the main house. Everyone else slept in places you rarely saw near the main house, because it was around the dinner table with dust on the floor that the drama took place.

The energy the Chases created in the kitchen was contagious. If someone wasn't there, they'd be coming soon, because it was general headquarters. The older children talked shop, and the younger ones did their homework and interrupted. It was a show of family life Americans didn't live anymore. It couldn't be recreated anywhere in the USA. You were offered more of the richest foods there than you could ever possibly eat. Kate's breads melted in your mouth, while Hester's cheeses were strong and sharp, and her milk was guzzled at every meal. She had straw blonde hair, milked the cows, made cheese, and slept on a haystack near the barn.

I ate the purest tomato I ever ate at that table. It squirted into my mouth radiant and alive as the most vital salsa, a tomato without any of the crispness or greenness of the kind at supermarkets, but fresh from the garden, as were all the vegetables they ate. Tomatoes, cheeses, bread, salsa, a slice of ham, that's what I remember for lunch. Dinner was a pot of beans, tortillas, fish, meat, potatoes, coffee, wine, and two helpings each. "Martha, get Seth some more wine... Get him some more beans, he didn't get enough beans... Get him some potatoes."

The September air was warm and Hal was usually jovial around dinnertime. If he wanted the evening to go past dinner, he'd pour you some wine when you weren't looking. The Chases made their own and kept it in a cellar by the nuthouse, the coolest place to be in the heat, and the closest thing to cave-like air-conditioning on the farm. Hal would keep a jug of the "family vino" by the side of the table on the floor near his chair and reach down for it during the course of the night, drinking it out of a coffee cup as he spoke.

"The stock market is just pure thought and doesn't exist," said Hal, "and when we run out of thoughts the economy will collapse."

If Hal didn't want to talk much after dinner, if something had gone wrong in the day, or someone in the family fell sick, he'd end the discussion on his terms. He'd feed you and you'd talk a little but it would be distracted and the night would end. Casey and I would take the mile and a half walk back to Kiler Canyon road using flashlights, though the Chases could find their way barefoot in the dark. Then we'd read by a kerosene lamp, go to sleep, and start another day of nothing.

"Just gimme plenty of bad books to read and I'll be fine," said Casey, and it wasn't hard, considering the house in town was better than most second-hand bookstores.

Casey and I were in Paso Robles to finish the project. That was Hal's rule to Casey: finish what you start. One of his favorite sayings to his children was "No Fun" (I imagine the old man saying it with a twinkle in his steely blue eyes, mouth crinkling under his glacial beard), because to Hal work was life. It was a point he made over and over to Casey and me as we sat at his long wooden table eating meat, beans, potatoes, and cheese and drinking wine or coffee. The great difference between Hal and his beatnik friends, and Hal and Casey, was that the foxy old man behind the beard thought fun was something bought on luxury time a working man couldn't afford. Art was a byproduct of uselessness and didn't solve any of life's problems.

"You can't understand why I didn't read any of their work after 1949?" he said to me in his high whiny voice, as distinctive as an instrument. "Why did I want to read about Jack's (Kerouac) depression on a mountain? Why did I want them hanging around trying to score drugs while I was busy building boats?"

While he was talking, Kate, his eldest daughter, was busy baking bread. Tubloq was carving a piece of wood with a knife trying to make up a game, and Barca was kicking him under the table. Martha listened attentively and the sky was blue outside, no sound of traffic or voices out the window, only wind and silence.

"You don't understand," Hal said again.

Casey looked on. I sat stunned, having walked into the conversation late, and Jenny, with beautiful dark skin like an Indian, sat beside me. She started Martha on a conversation about mental institutions of the 1600s. I could see Hal was glad to have the subject changed, though he had a bothered look in his eyes.

"Wasn't writing Jack's work?" I asked.

"Yes, it was. Writing was his work, and building boats was mine."

Casey and I were staying a mile and a half away up Kiler Canyon but still on Chase property and a hill climb up from Quill's cabin was the nuthouse where the Chase's kept the almonds they shook off the trees. On the upper deck of the nuthouse lived a silent powerful son of Hal's, Mal. To the side of the nuthouse was a 36-foot boat Quill was building. Kate and

10year-old Barca showed me around it one afternoon.

It was here Jenny and I had one of our first real breakdowns as our own early love was shattering in the first months of fall. Jenny, Casey, his kids, and I all visited the farm for a week in mid-August before the project had transitioned from Santa Cruz to Paso Robles, a three hour drive south on highway 101. Jenny and I slept on a haystack outside of Quill's cabin under the moon, and thought we saw a UFO. We made love in the nuthouse and somewhere else on the hillside when she asked me if she was smart enough for me one morning. I don't know if it was the trees or the sky, but I told her I loved her and of course she was, because I had the dreamiest, steamiest conversations I ever had in my life with Jenny. She didn't believe me because she didn't know where our relationship was going, or maybe she did, but I didn't know, and it made life none the easier when I returned to Paso Robles several weeks later. I remember having to pull over at a rest stop at dusk, 10 miles from town near an abandoned army barracks, to write something in my journal (a black and white composition book) about the horrible shit Jenny and I were going through as lovers. Me leaving her in Santa Cruz, ditching my room, uncertain of our future, to embark on a mad literary project. None of it made sense.

"I can only be responsible for myself," I tried to think at the time, but someone was always watching me as I was trying to watch me at the long wooden table eating supper.

Hal's fears weren't my fears. He was a product of Columbia University, Ivy League, first as an undergraduate with Jack Kerouac and Allen Ginsberg, then as a graduate student studying anthropology. He went onto a professorship at the University of Colorado, I think, the western state he came from. But his philosophy or some aspect of it, maybe its idealism, must have been too radical for the university and he split to make his life on a farm.

Hal's view on the State envisioned one state rising against another in the early 2000s and fighting for control of the Union. A newspaper addict, Hal did the crossword puzzle every day and read the news section over and over to figure out the lies of semantics. He had visions of the fall of America constantly. He grew up in its rise, for God's sake, so who better to see it fall? And, when it falls, watch out! Hal moved to the country to build his ark and raise his children by the stream.

"If an intelligence doesn't react to its immediate surroundings, what worth is it, Seth?"

No TVs on Hal's farm, no radio, no refrigerator. An electric lightbulb in the main house to read and talk to by night, old car engines in the front, and one little clock by Hal's head ticking away. This was what blew me away most when I saw his farm for the first time – his family didn't look like they were living in this century, yet his lifestyle, from his family's perspective, was the most ordinary way of life. They seemed to find purpose in every action they set their minds to, whether it be baking bread, fixing an engine, building a boat, killing a pig (then the feeling was sadness; Quill shot it and they hung it by the barn) or hiring themselves out as nut farmers for neighboring farms. At no time did reality ever seem to be so deeply questioned as to stop anyone in the family from performing their task.

    In fact, quite the opposite happened. After dinner the family heads talked shop, planning and preparing for tomorrow as carefully, concisely, and thoroughly as they could, while the little ones played. Each member of the working family (between six and nine people, three went to school) would have their daily assignment of chores they were to meet, and because the chores were directly related to the way they were living (on a farm), their purpose was not abstract. They weren't aimlessly driving to the store looking for milk and cheese (Hester and the cows gave them that), or job hunting from a paper whose society didn't relate to them. Hal was living outside of society in nature, feeding off nature, and his kids were natural byproducts fulfilling their roles.

Hal built his life from all the philosophy books he read. I still remember going into Martha's house in town. She was born and raised in Paso Robles, pronounced "Ro-bels" by the natives. It was her parents' house and the entire place was stacked with books, every room. Only books lived in the house. In a private den off the living room, secured by a door, were Hal's books he'd had as a young man. There were stacked shelves of Thomas Wolfe, Nietzsche, an autographed copy of Kerouac's *The Town and the City* signed "John Kerouac." It was the only book he ever read by his friend and he was adamant *The Town and the Country* was the correct title, even though Casey argued with him over it at the kitchen table.

Hal had books of Indian tribes next to books on the physiological effects of sleep. There was some of the strangest, most obscure knowledge the world has ever known there. I wish I'd written down at least some of the titles; they were sitting right under my nose Casey couldn't get over the Kerouac inscription, while I had a sudden flash that all the books had created Hal's mind. His move to the country to become a peasant (he'd call himself a peasant under his white beard, a twinkle in his eye, white worn work shirt on, cup of wine in his hand) was created by what he had read. He knew all too well that he wasn't born a peasant. All the photographs of him in New York with Jack Kerouac, Allen Ginsberg, William S. Burroughs and who else, portrayed a thin romantic wearing an overcoat, slacks, dress shoes, and a clean-shaven face. The picture of a young dashing intellectual scholar, not a peasant farmer living in the rolling hills 30 miles off the California coast.

It was clear Hal Chase had put tons of bullshit behind him to reach his current plateau of existence. He all but became a nut in a shell, as myth had it, not leaving his property for 10 years, sitting at his study table watching the sun rise and fall, seeing his children grow. They were the key to his sanity and the world Hal created for himself, the exponents of his mind that trigger- flashed incessantly through whatever doubts or misgivings he must have had about existence. Hal lived as noble and proud as he knew how, and the reflection of his royalty in blood and spirit tended the land and kept the old man company in the evening around beans, meat, salsa, tortillas, cowboy coffee, and cheap beer or homemade wine His children were the meaning of the existence Hal created and he'd given them all the power and strength of the most enduring life on the planet. He'd given them the mind to fix machines. He'd given his children dirt roads and felt the people from LA were overtaking Paso Robles. "Pave the roads – all the people from Los Angeles want to do is pave the roads," he'd say. "It's the first thing they do when they move here. Then they build a water slide."

"It's gettin' to be like San Luis Abysmal," said Tubloq.

Hal gave his children – all except the first born lived on Chase property or nearby – a life without TV, radio, tape player, refrigerator, dishwasher, or automatic laundry machine (they had a hand-cranked one). All of Hal's books lead him to the conclusion it was best to live as a Mexican farmer with a funky family to live for, care for, and breathe through. All of the books in the world were made of words that couldn't breathe the concrete life Hal was obviously looking for in the country. The life of the peasant, dirt and soil. "The peasant is eternal," Oswald Spengler wrote in *The Decline of the West,* a book Hal exhorted on me, saying he, Jack and Burroughs all used it as a model to study society. I wanted to read most everything Hal highly recommended to me – *The Rise and Fall of the Roman Empire*, anything by Nietzsche, *The Red and the Black* by Stendhal – so many books Casey had to remind me I was staying on the farm to work on X. That was my visa into the incredible life I was allowed to witness from day to day. Being the dutiful servant I was, fresh out of college at 25 (only a few years late), and realizing Hal was a true patron of the arts, I listened to Casey. But Hal's reading list never left my mind.

The first time I met the man, Flaubert's *Sentimental Education* was sitting on the table near his hand. I mentioned I started it once, liked it, but couldn't finish it. In his high goat-like voice Hal said, "I'm not surprised, it's a depressing book."

Being the peasant he became, built from all he read, Hal had a stature that was hard to see around. He was king at the head of a table in a country he created, a nutshell he kept perfectly closed. When Casey entered the picture his very existence, based on '60s drug use, beatnik memories, loose sex, and fun (Casey often said he arrived in 1967, the summer of love) was a challenge. This 60 year-old artist from the outside, slicked back black hair, young body and mind, nourished and frightened Hal simultaneously. The farm was an inside world few strangers questioned.

I was a student on the scene and no threat. My presence caused only minor tremors in the psyche of the collective. Since I was intelligent I could often keep up with Hal's thoughts. I remember one evening, the house darkening, he explained to Casey and me why baseball was the only organized sport that reflected a non-selfish bargaining agreement between people. An insane conversation in which Casey and I would bring up the similarities between basketball, football and baseball, and a missing time clock had nothing to do with Hal's argument. It had something to do with the relationship between the first and second basemen. Casey listened for a good hour as Hester the milkmaid, always so serious and smart, prodded her head in agreement with her dad, looking at me several times in disbelief, unable to comprehend how I couldn't see the simple non-reciprocal arrangements infielders made with each other when they threw the ball. Casey didn't get it either.

We talked about modern historical figures too. The old man really couldn't get over Ronald Reagan. To Hal, Reagan was the end of an America he'd been watching fall for decades. Hal hated him with every tooth left in his mouth.

"It really is absurd when you think of people paying money to sit in a dark movie theater for a couple of hours and then we elect a B movie actor for president," said Hal. "Can you believe it?"

"What was the last movie you saw?" asked Casey, who was famous for seeing more movies than anyone. We used to watch cheap double features at a theater on the beach in Capitola, right outside of Santa Cruz, a couple of times a week, with a popcorn sculpture of the owner in the ancient lobby. "*The Vikings* with Kirk Douglas." "That was 1958," said Casey.

"Nothing's changed," said Hal.

I could believe Reagan was the president, but I didn't know how to say this to Hal. I was raised in LA (so was Casey) and understood the power of movies. Movie stars were the Gods of modern America but Hal knew that; he was the one who taught me that celebrity was a commodity.

"Do you really think in 10 or 20 years state will rise against state in a battle for sovereignty?" I asked.

Hal shook his fist like an old Bible preacher and from his seat in Paso RoblesUSA: "Yes, no one thought the Soviet Union would fall as soon as it did, and they don't have movie stars for presidents!" I agreed, but still couldn't believe that in 10 years the world was going to blow.

Who knows the fate of mankind? From the property Hal never left, he spent his old age making musical instruments he never played (harps, lyres) on a worktable off his house under an oak tree – medieval instruments he'd build and sell. Hal didn't go into Paso Robles for 10 years, not a 10-minute paved drive from his house, but sat at a table each day reading the newspaper and thinking about it, talking to his wife and children as they came and left for work.

Paso Robles was a small old American town with a park in the middle, swings and a library, shops from the 1950s and bars circling the park, where little nuts dropped from the trees and hit me on the head. It's easy to say that Hal saw nothing good for the future of America or the world and in his own way was declaring it. Hal thought America lived all wrong. Or, I should say, at Hal's I thought America must've had a choice at some point in its existence, a way it could go, and it chose cheap housing and enough pavement from coast to coast to circle the earth 10 times over (a fact I'm sure would spark Hal with wonder at the madness of it all). If only America didn't individuate (Hal's word) but became close-knit communities not so reliant on mass consumption but more able to consume from the land, live off the land as families working to cultivate each other's superior self, it would have been a nation to make the world proud.

    I remember looking off a ridge with Quill near the nuthouse to a housing development on the other side of the freeway. Quill pointed with his finger and said, "The cancer." And there was Tubloq, who wore a black cape to his first day of seventh grade, and had long blonde hair and a dirty face. Tubloq must've been Holden Caulfield in another life, the smartest smart-ass kid I ever met. He'd carve incredible Rubik's Cube-like games with a knife and wood and was interested in everything (he told me I was a member of the family once, and it felt so good). Or Kate, the daughter made of stone, who smiled, baked bread, walked barefoot (not pregnant), worked in the field, and stayed near her dad. She also sang folk songs, had clear, strong, blue eyes and seemed like she'd never have a nervous breakdown in her life. People like trees and stone, children and younger children, who could run the farm by themselves if they had to. They all had bodies like lumberjacks.

Hal had given his children life and said, "Here are the trees, the sky, and the tarantulas." (Once Tubloq picked one up from under the kitchen table and carried it outside.) "Here's the UFOs, if you want to believe in them. Here's books and conversations and the only media that gets in is the newspaper with all its lies, and I'll tell you what it's lying about I'll show you, I'll read articles out loud in disbelief and wonder at the stupidity of my countrymen – gasp at the decay of the world, my world, I give to you. And in consequence you give to me."

Hal will close his eyes one night knowing he's given Paso Robles kings, but until that night he'll work and work hard. Hal's first born, Eric, the one who got away and became a carpenter in Marin (a very touchy subject for Hal), was a Superman himself, racing boats in world-championship events. Hal always told Eric "No fun." It was his slogan. Hal said it to all of his kids when they were young, and how they listened and took his words to heart! They worked their bodies into a race of people that could rule the earth with benevolence and wisdom. They were a group that was meant to take charge at the proper fork in the road when America was changing course (the late 1800s) but got pronged by the industrial revolution instead. To the America that could have been, Hal was a relic.

Of course, his genes could never multiply quickly enough. There were only nine children and they were having children slowly (only two grandchildren for Martha and Hal – none when I was there). It came out as the month went on that Hal had a strong prejudice against a Flemish people whose blood mixed with Scandinavians (I can't really remember the mixture but it was something equally bizarre). Casey thought it strange too. It was the reason Hal gave for disliking Hannah's boyfriend at the time, the preacher's son. Hal was so hard on his daughters' suitors that he was certainly building a master race in his mind. Casey corroborated this to an extent, or he at least thought that Hal's life was an anthropology experiment he created for himself to master.

It was easy on the farm to have diabolical visions of what Hal was up to, especially since he told Casey and me we were in denial about being Jewish. Any genius embodies sorcerer-like powers and Hal's peasant life was hard to battle against. To Casey and me, Hal preached that art was a dead end. When I countered by saying art was exciting, he said: "I'm sure it's exciting. I don't doubt it's exciting. But where does it leave you? All you can do is develop a cult of personality."

In the end, Hal saw the life of the artist as leading only to madness, and there sat Casey, 60 years old and mad. It could only be made on luxury time, he reasoned, while the work the world required was done by healthier people. All that luxury time had its roots in decadence. Art was created out of a profound boredom. Hal said that he and Jack Kerouac had endless conversations about how Jack wrote out of boredom, Burroughs wrote out of boredom, and how they were all bored out of their minds. At the same time, Casey was working on a book about a dead drinking friend of his who believed that his boredom was superior to anyone else's. How genius and boredom walked hand in hand.

Hal thought that the only thing an artist ended up doing to himself was cultivating his personality, and once done all they could be known for in the 20th century was the personality they created and cultivated through their art. If this was all it amounted to, why bother? Once society could see you, once it could label you and tout you as something recognizable to all, then you were dead. You couldn't grow, you couldn't become anything but an image of yourself, making an artist an incredibly lonely person.

Hal thought writing would destroy him. I remember him soberly contemplating the reality of writing every day, and he shook in fear saying, "I couldn't do that," and I believed him. Hal also said he tried re-reading Dostoevsky's books, checked out from the public library, but couldn't get into them, even though he loved them as a young man. I wondered if the same thing would happen to me one day, if I'd change my conception of reality so much I could no longer touch what was once closest to my heart.

    Hal turned his life into art and didn't want to look back. Yet he opened his door to Casey. He let in an outsider. Hal and Casey name dropped characters from Marin in the '60s all night long. They didn't know of each other before, but shared similar memories because they lived in the same county at the same time.

Casey was a broken man after Anne dumped him. I'm sure if he could've he would've drank himself to death ("Jews can't drink, only smoke weed," he said). He would've committed suicide as quickly as a cat running up a tree. I'm sure Casey wanted to end his life, but he had two kids from Anne (Hal called Casey's ex "a mall rat") and they kept him going.

Casey wouldn't say one word to me all day when we were staying in a cabin in the meadows of Paso Robles, alone and together with nothing to do but talk all day. I'd read a book, or read Casey's book, take a short walk up a hill to the nuthouse, and watch the sun grow increasingly hot by the hour. Paso Robles was going through a heatwave and it was over

100 degrees outside – tarantula weather, Indian summer, flies and yellow jackets circling the cabin, and we said nothing to each other all day. We worked on the book only about a week out of the three I was there. It was looking impossible to complete it.

It was best when we talked about the manuscript with Hal. He thought John Stephens (X), the anti-hero of Casey's book, was a fictional character the minute Casey decided to write about him, and that blew Casey's mind. He played with his devilishly black and gray beard at Hal's table, eyes peering, and repeated over and over how incredible it was that X, his friend, had become fictional

When Hal went off on Casey about how art (Casey's 60-year life) was a dead end and that Casey didn't have his kids to support him while Hal's were playing like kangaroos around the wooden table, it must've been too much for Casey to bear. He was obviously weak in the face of Hal's superior life (I was too), and several times lost his cool in the cabin, saying Hal was really starting to piss him off.

Casey's lust for Hal's 17year-old daughter, Hannah, compounded the problems between the two. She wanted to be a poet (one of her poems hung on the wall above Hal's head) and was obviously taken with Casey's poetic artistic life. Casey was in awe of her youth and the fictional wonder of the entire seduction. He saw the three daughters as the three muses, and while there did a painting of them as such. Casey must've felt like a character himself, and fell in love with Hannah imagining her howling at the moon for him on a warm September night.

    I slept on the top bunk reading Chinese poetry by a kerosene lamp, dreaming of coming home to Jenny. I spent my days taking walks and sometimes jacking off in the fields. Every day around six or seven I'd walk to Hal's in the twilight orange and dark fading blue. It was a mile and a half up Kiler Canyon, by a winding creek under oak trees for miles of it, then onto Hal's property, under many more trees and an easy to follow path. I was often stoned (Casey and I wouldn't always talk, but we'd get stoned) thinking any thought I wanted 'till I came to the house for dinner, past the rope swing and the barn with the cows and the horses.

In private, Hal confided to me he wasn't trying to destroy Casey; he knew he was weak, but he liked argumentation (like Socrates) and was only trying to argue art with Casey because he understood it to be his favorite subject. I understood and ate some of Hester's cheese.

In society, the rules were reversed from how they were on the farm. Hal didn't believe in luxury items or making time stop and start on principle alone. He let time rise, fall, and scatter as it would. Hal knew society wouldn't allow for its citizens to think like him and be free men of ideology. His disgust with impending 21st century America was so extreme he was scared to leave his property. Sometimes at dinner, Mexican laborers would visit and sing folk songs in Spanish, playing guitar. Kate would join in and Hal would beam. It was a wonder he spoke English at all. The laborers were given as much food and wine as they wanted. One of them, Enrique, was to father Hester's baby a few years later.

Through all of this, Martha was one of the most solid humans I ever met. She listened carefully and considerately to whatever Hal said, and stood over the stove most of the day, cooking three huge meals for the family to eat and savor. Martha was a Paso Robles woman and was obviously the family's anchor. She was very warm in greeting, a few hairs sticking out of her chin, and was the opposite of the American female concern over her appearance every moment of the day. She wore thick glasses and a polyester off-white T-shirt with a big chest pocket. She probably hadn't worn makeup for 20 or 30 years, if ever. The Chases were not the beautiful people of the city, who have all turned themselves into replicas of glittering Roman statues, showing off to each other in apartments and lofts. They were people of the earth, made of potatoes, meat, sun, work and more work, with certain pleasures at the end of the day. Their thoughts always came back to the running of the farm, how to maintain it and help it grow. Who was going to fix the generator, who was going to run an errand in town? Solid thoughts about survival, not twisting, out-of-control thoughts, suicidal thoughts, but certain ones. There was always work to be done, and they arranged it, did it, ate, and loved each other.

    I wasn't raised in the country. If my work could keep me distracted and healthy and I could see it as a constant project of my life, making my farm my art, my family my art, my wife my art, would there be any need for art at all? If my life became so realized that the

Hamlet question I've taken to define my being disappeared, would I exist? If I could build up my body from the decimated point art has left it, I could live in Hal's shoes and marvel at my ability to grab reality by the balls and get down to the sweaty innards of the thing.

Hal did it. He chose his spot. He put his little finger on the map and moved his family south from Marin figuring he could live as he chose in Paso Robles without invoking the wrath of the town (or so he tried). All he wanted was to fit in with himself and his conceptions. From there his children would fall like nuts from the trees. They'd wear non-ironed white shirts, and stick out at school as odd rustic folk, but Hal didn't care. It seemed to be his objective to stretch the First Amendment as far as he could, because the family mimicked no one but themselves. Hal Chase was the zealot of an American religion from which he'd distilled only the purest aspects: working hard for your money, having children and keeping the family together, and exchanging goods and services with your neighbor for the sake of community. Hal did not necessarily put a financial burden on every transaction.

The Chases never spoke badly about others (except politicians) nor did they lose themselves in idle gossip over movie and rock stars. They didn't know who anyone was. Hal saw hero worship as a way society took away power from the individual, and he was clearly interested in harnessing all the power he could for himself, his family and his land.

I remember saying to Hal the day before

I left, "I feel great after I play basketball or have a good day of writing."

Hal nodded and said, "That's good you enjoy playing basketball and writing. Society tries to take that away from you every chance it gets." Hal realized I wasn't about to live his life. He told me after Paso Robles that I should travel, meet people, and write about my experiences. That's what Jack did. His books weren't novels, he said, they were recollections, and I decided then and there to travel to New Orleans.

I listened, happy to hear a man speak my thoughts. Hal wanted to escape the evils of the empire, but he fought his war on his soil like an old Civil War general.

Casey was fighting his war against

America too, but had no property to show for it. His was fought on the run in rented rooms and vans. At 60, Casey was trying to raise his children for the first time and he was doing it without a home. Casey's warfare against evil was more self-destructive than Hal's. He was fueled by a reservoir of hostility, often against himself, and a desire for invisibility that bordered on absolute paranoia.

    I remember once in Santa Cruz going to Casey's and Anne's house and Casey had all the doors shut. He was peering nervously out of closed blinds to make sure I wasn't Manuel Neri, a known California sculptor who'd promised to come over to look at Casey's paintings and maybe buy one. Casey took a deep breath when he saw it was me, gave me a toke, and said, "Let's get out of here before I sell anything."

We left to see a movie (*Naked Lunch*, ironically) and on the walk to the theater down the Santa Cruz streets, past the barking dogs Casey hated, he told me of the painters Chaim Soutine and Oscar Kokoschka. Casey told me I had to get to know them and being the good student I was, I tried.

"Kokoschka told me I was a writer not a painter, but I'm not so sure he'd say that now," said Casey, "or maybe he would since he only liked it if you painted like him."

Casey's philosophy was "Art and money don't mix." He hated selling anything, and rarely did. This appealed to Hal, because he saw in Casey a rebel against the State. But to

Hal, Casey's form of rebellion was adolescent. It required he live off government money, women's money, or parents' money. Hal was a rebel too and I remember him once screaming at me, standing up from the table, bending near the sink, that the people who wore ties, suits and black leather shoes were the most enslaved of all. Hal raised his voice when he said this in his peasant clothes, regal white hair, powerful body, and I listened as I never had before. Hal thought Casey hadn't done all he could for himself.

Remembering New York as Hal remembered it (circa 1940s), he told Casey and me stories of painters who literally carried their canvases down Fifth Avenue to sell to whoever would or could buy. Casey would stare in disbelief, and Hal with the big wart on his nose like an ancient medicine man would insist on his advice in utter seriousness.

Once, Casey tried to put on Hal by giving him a book of philosophy called *By the Late John Brockman.* Casey bought it for a dollar at Logo's, a Santa Cruz used bookstore, and it had themes such as "man is dead," "every movie is the first movie," and it contained myriad epigrams written in a language so cryptic and over-serious it made Casey, Jenny, me, and anyone else who read it laugh. But Hal wouldn't laugh, even though Casey put a sticker on the cover saying "You'll never be the same after you read this." Hal didn't go for the joke. He tried to seriously discuss the book with us at dinner, not smiling for a moment as he nodded his head saying he got a lot out of it, and agreed with the author, Brockman, that "man is dead." Casey sat on the bench of the kitchen table smiling, shaking his head, and mumbling to himself, unable to believe what Hal was doing. I'm sure Casey thought it was the old man's way of gaining power. Hal was making us question what we only dared laugh at, because he really believed "man is dead."

    That's not to say Hal didn't laugh at things he found funny. He smiled all the time at puns others made, clever phrases, or perceptive thoughts. But he was a general and so was Casey and, after discussing their similarities, all they could do was analyze their differences. Hal's life, his art, could immediately be seen and felt. It was regenerating itself daily in the farm. Casey's territory was more abstract, and lay in the land of poetry and painting. Since he had given up on society long ago, not working a job since he was 32, Casey's art was only seen by himself and a few others. And, because Casey's life was falling apart, he questioned the worth of his life's work on Hal's farm. Casey let Martha insulate him (her words) with pork fat and beans while he sat playing with his beard, listening to Hal rip poetry apart. It must've made Casey wonder if he'd ever written a poem in his life. Casey's unrequited love for Hannah and his disquieted spirit were a battle for Hal. The outside world was not often let into his 1800's shack. I think that Hal's being a patron to us as Casey worked on the manuscript was a first and last for the old man.

A gracious act, it spoke of Hal's need to assist a poet. He trusted an artist enough to let him on his land, breathe his marijuana smoke in private and his thoughts of reality in public at the table. Hal saw Casey needed the work to get him through his troubled times, and did all that was possible to make it happen. Whatever Hal's perception of art, I know he looked at it as work not unlike building boats, or any private endeavor. Like any project it took time, dedication, and space.

Hal once described to me his perfect idea of the world as one where people were allowed to perform the tasks they were suited for, as if we were all blessed by destiny. In his heart, Hal knew the pain of looking in the want ads and finding nothing in his community to feed him. He had been a door-to-door encyclopedia salesman, and told me of how he despised it. Hal believed in poetry as if some people were meant to play it, seeing it as music, and had faith in Casey to play it, and Casey had faith in me to read through thousands of pages looking for gold.

"Are you sure Seth is the appointed one?" Hal asked Casey before I arrived. "I think he's afraid of falling in the crapper."

"He may be but I can tell by his laugh if the manuscript is funny, and by his hollow laugh if he's grok'd it. He's the chosen one."

Of course, Casey wanted to know about the Beat Hal, once he found out this was the man who was best friends with Jack Kerouac 50 years ago. Hal lived in New York City, did drugs, and had long conversations with William

S. Burroughs, his wife Joan (Hal said she gave the Beats their humor), and Allen Ginsberg. They were all roommates.

"One day Allen came in and said, 'I'm a poet,'" recalled Hal, "and I said, 'Great! You're a poet, now do the dishes!'"

Casey wanted the Hal who had introduced Neal Cassady to Jack Kerouac, the Hal history would remember through biopics and writing. The mythical Hal who was a character in the changing and shaping of 20th century American literature. Yet so much of Hal's life – his boat building, his farm and family – was an attempt to escape from his historical role. He wanted to stay invisible. But Casey wanted to catch him, and maybe Hal wanted to be caught, but not like Casey did it.

Casey wanted to hear every Jack Kerouac story he could because he loved Jack's poetry and was obsessed by the trajectory of Kerouac's life, the fame and self-destruction, society killing an artist, and the ways X paralleled Jack. Hal's past was not a topic he talked about with his children, wife or neighbors. It was the obvious point of attack – the most obviously intriguing thing about this aged patriarch sitting at his wooden table, drinking his home-made wine, weaving his home-made shoes, and tending to his homemade children. There Casey was, Beat journalist on the biggest story of his life, and there sat Hal, talking about the first beatnik he ever met, a man named Banjo who went off to live with nothing but a guitar in the Rocky Mountains. One afternoon, Hal told of Jack

Kerouac's relationship with his college football coach, Lou Little. As Hal spoke, I saw the gray New York City football field and the white chalk marks. Jack was at Columbia to be a football star but he and Lou Little didn't get along, and Jack's failure to make it good with the team broke his sports writer father's heart. Hal said Jack was irrevocably crushed by letting his father down. Jack's dad wanted nothing more than to see his son be a great football player, and now he was a writer? Hal also told of how fast Kerouac typed once football was over, how he heard the return smash all night long, how Jack was a Canuck and how this alienated him as a child in Lowell.

Hal once described his memories going off like flashbulbs and Casey kept him blinking on topics that were obviously taboo in the Chase home. The children knew who their dad had been, but they didn't know much, and hadn't even seen some of the famous photographs taken of him.

One day at lunch Hal said to Casey and me, "I know what 'Naked Lunch' means, do you?"

Barca and Tubloq, the two youngest, stared speechless. Casey and I looked to Hal for an answer but he said nothing. Instead, he stared us down.

At the time I wondered what Casey was doing talking about the beatnik days all the time. I now see he was baiting Hal and Hal probably wanted to be baited. He wanted to expose his life to Casey and me so someone on the outside could get it right; but who could do that? Hal must have seen himself being poorly portrayed in biography after biography of Jack Kerouac or Allen Ginsberg. Now he was going to tell Casey and me that his friends were friends and he was a king. All any of them were doing with their time was looking for a way to die, but he was looking for a way to live Hal's life proved it, his work proved it, and so did theirs. He, Kerouac, Ginsberg and Burroughs had come from the same tree but grown in different directions. I listened, but didn't start conversations about the Beats. I was uncomfortable talking about a subject I felt irritated Hal. I let Casey do that for me.

The mealtime scenes on the farm were bred of familiarity and understanding – "pass the potatoes, the bread, the beans, the steak," came a chorus of voices at once. The children's hands and bowls shuffled across the table wildly. No one waited for anyone else to eat, and if you were hungry (and they were) you ate what was on the table. You didn't worry if you were eating the last bite of a dish because there was always more to eat. Kate, the oldest daughter, once told me that if it doesn't get eaten it just goes bad, and Hal nodded in agreement, and everyone drank Hester's milk. Many times the Chases mentioned how they hated store-bought milk, how it was like a different product entirely, and drinking it made me feel I had never tasted real milk before. No one talked about the food they were eating, they just ate.

In Casey's and Hal's battle, if indeed I've even begun to describe the love/hate nature of the two, one issue that divided them was sex. Whatever one's take on Casey, and he could be a terrifying man, bent on destroying and subverting the world around him, he wasn't shy when it came to talking about his sexual exploits. Casey said more than once that sex, drugs, and not working were his keys to making art. And Hal, well, Hal in his puritan way was uncomfortable around the topics of sex or drugs because they were both sins from a world he'd dipped his finger into, and now he was washing them clean. Hal had to protect his children. Yet Casey, with his lust for Hal's youngest daughter (if not all three) put sex right on the table, and Hal flipped.

Casey noticed this weakness and exploited it. One day (I wasn't there but I always imagined this conversation taking place by the workshop outside the tool shed), Hal told Casey that Allen Ginsberg and William S. Burroughs weren't really gay. Allen Ginsberg was just play acting, affecting a sophisticated New York City manner, while William S. Burroughs was schizophrenic and being a "fag" was just one of his 13 personalities. Beyond disbelief, Casey asked Hal over and over if he'd ever read the Ginsberg poem, *Please Master*, but he hadn't. It didn't matter anyway. Hal knew the truth, and we didn't.

Most afternoons, Casey lay on the lower bunk, flies circling him, and he'd read a dime-store novel to get him through the day. Either that, or he'd sit outside the cabin in the sun on a well-lit morning and flip through dozens of old art magazines, looking at pictures. There were piles of them and he'd read the stories over and over, and occasionally make me read him something aloud. I remember reading a description of Soutine's painting attack on the canvas, how he ripped it up. Casey screamed "Yeah!" and cheered his hero on as I read. More often than not, it was Casey's book on X I was reading aloud. That's how we went through the editing process of our work, sitting at a kitchen table in Quill's bare but beautiful cabin up Kiler Canyon road, the door of the cabin open before us and armies of wild turkeys passing by. Yellow jackets swirled outside in the sun near the showerhead, the woodstove was behind us, and there were two shelves of cooking supplies, although neither one of us cooked much, or even knew how.

It was clear Casey wanted me to be more than an editor. He wanted a maid, a chauffeur and a cohort to boot, but that was asking too much. I was off, and destroying my car, for what? To one day write about my Paso Robles experience? I was going out of my head to help Casey, but he wanted to starve, so I made some terrible-tasting beans (let the beans soak?), and atrocious cowboy coffee – just threw the grounds into boiling water. Often we'd eat ham, avocado, cheese, tomatoes or anything the Chases gave us from dinner the night before. We'd have to eat it fast, though, because there was no refrigeration and the ham tasted sweaty and warm the next day. Our vegetable sandwiches could taste good, but they were never filling enough. Nothing was until dinner.

We ran out of dope in the three weeks I was there, a sin for two potheads. I remember Casey sitting in the living room off the kitchen wearing only shorts, scraping a bowl by his bed, saying we were going to get real high on resin, and we did. We talked about the book and I looked through boxes and boxes of X material. Everything was kept in cardboard boxes; the book was being made on the run. There were photographs of John Stephens, many in fact, because Casey was a photographer in the '60s and had the first one-man show at the San Francisco Museum of Art, photographing the whole fuckin' decade as memorably as anyone. There were little memo books X used to carry around, complete with lists, doodles, songs and quotes. The hero of the book never had a pad, yet used to make notes on Di Fabrizio shoes and his favorite kinds of ties. This from a revolutionary? Pieces of paper X left drawings on, simple line drawings, that Casey liked a lot. One was of an angry-looking man staring straight from the page saying, "Nobody needs you" or "You're better off forgetting about me." We were searching, trying to explain X's many personalities and how to make sense of them in a book, while we were living a larger-than-life novel acted out by the entire Chase family on their property.

What can I say about the manuscript sometimes called *Me Vale Madre*, a title that described X's fuck-it attitude towards life, or *On We*. It was 1000 or so interchangeable pages, and each page had its own poem, diary, or letter. All of it theoretically to X, but not all of it was. Sometimes it drifted in Casey's head and I couldn't do anything but read it, laugh or not laugh, and tell him what to cut and keep on each page. The problem was the individual pages weren't making a whole. The thing was a monster beyond anyone's ability to tame. Casey didn't know what to do with it, or how to present X. Once he said he wanted to go the *Let Us Now Praise Famous Men* route and put everything in, good or bad, and put the photos in too, and the tapes. Because the book was so sprawling it was impossible to break it down.

Madness or genius, who knew, but when the 1000 pages were stacked like a mountain before you, and you were staring them down, they lived and had integrity. What Casey wanted from me was to select his best pages, cull the gold, and gather them into a group. In my own egghead way I did this by pen, marking each page, and trying to tell Casey which scenes and ideas to expand on. After I read every page, I knew my job was done. As Hal said, "It's not your book, Seth, it's Casey's book."

To Casey the book was the culmination of his 60-year life. Casey used to say that whenever you asked any guy what he was doing in the '60s he was always working on a book and how he never wanted to be like one of those guys, but now the joke was on him. X was Jew-baiting Casey from beyond the grave for even trying to write about him!

Old-age Casey, drawer, doodler, and oil painter in 1993, who kept his life in a series of boxes, the collected crap of the last 60 years, was falling down. The book on John Stephens, alias X, was the most important, deepest and funniest work of art Casey's life called for, and its failure was a testament to his shortcomings, because if it wasn't funny it was a flop. Casey agonized for days how it wasn't funny enough, it just wasn't funny enough. But Casey often said to me that a part of him never wanted the book to end, because what would he have to write about if it did?

I'd laugh because it was true. X was an elusive figure, hard to pin down and tie up as a fictional character standing for something, aside from falling down drunk. X's personality had so many contradictions it was lethal.

"Like a comet across the sky, X exploded," I read aloud. "He'd smoke your dope and complain at the same time. He lived in his suit and never took it off, not even during sex.

"X =

COMEDIAN

ITINERANT MUSICIAN

A LIFE OF VOLUNTARY POVERTY ("ALL GOLD IS FOOL'S GOLD")

ALCOHOLIC

FEMINIST

REVOLUTIONARY

MASTER BOGARTER AND FRIEND

OF THE NEAR-FAMOUS

HIGH SCHOOL FOOTBALL HERO

NAVY MAN WHO RE-UPPED
CON MAN

STORYWRITER POET

HOW MANY OF US ARE THERE?"

"This doesn't even begin to describe the angles of X," said Casey. "How could he re-up in the Navy? It was the squarest thing you could do, from the hippest dude. It was like Kerouac wearing his bathing suit in the hot baths in Big Sur. He was the hip king of the

Beats but oh, so square. And how do I transcribe Johnny's wheeze?"

One night Casey talked to Hal about the book. The light was growing dark blue but no one turned on the lights. Only Hal, Casey, and I sat at the table, a rare occurrence, and Hal got a little paranoid after Casey told a story about Johnny crashing on houseboats in Sausalito. He must have felt the ghost of X fly into the kitchen.

He said to Casey, "I'm not so sure John Stephens would like me. I'm sure he'd find fault with me."

As Hal spoke, two family members drifted through the kitchen, partly oblivious to what Hal was saying, and partly aware. They knew when the old man spoke, especially about personal matters, it wasn't their place to speak but to carry on with their chores.

"He wouldn't hate you, Hal."

"Why, Casey?"

"Because he'd respect you for being an iconoclast. He'd respect your ideals, your farm, and your renunciation."

Hal said nothing to that. He knitted his brows, took his eyes off Casey, and started another conversation. The ghost must have left him.

I had a vision of Paso Robles in the twilight blues. Kate and Hester were sitting on swings up the little footpath that led from the barn with its cows to the house, sharing a moment together as sisters, looking at the sunset glow orangeish white through the leaves of many oak trees, with cats, dogs and birds walking around. They looked like they'd been taken from this modern world of accelerated time and fast food, and placed in a more angelic setting. They were living out their angelic roles for the family to see, the sunlight playing on their black and golden hair, smiles on their faces, because living on the farm was no daydream for them, it was reality. Their father had given to them what he saw as right, and they accepted.

As Hal gave them life, he also took it away. Where could his children go but to the farm? As strong, healthy and naturally quick-minded as they were, their upbringing made it very difficult for them to ever leave and start a life on the outside. It was their father's rule. Only the oldest, Eric, got away and must've been worthy of a superhero. (I remember a Flash vs. Superman comic as a kid, the two racing the earth to see who would win.) Most of the children stayed on the farm, and all lived in the area. Quill and Hester are now raising their babies there, and I'm sure they birthed them there, too. If one of the kids needed stitches, Hal would stitch them up. Hannah Chase was the only one I couldn't see fitting easily into the life he gave her. She was driven intellectually – working, cooking and planning wasn't her idea of a life. Her head was up her ass in 18th century poetry, not the harvest, and Hal had a poem of hers hanging on the wall above his head, a certified award from Paso Robles High stamped on it. Hannah was trying to get a scholarship out of that school; she excelled there, but Hal was hard on her in her pursuits. At dinner one night, Hannah mentioned the name of a college she wanted to attend to study poetry. Hal asked her how the music program was. She didn't know. "Poetry is music," he said. "You can't take the two apart."

    Barca was the other Chase who stood out strangely, but it was because he was the youngest and wild beyond control. When I was there he was seven years old and would play rough games under the table, kicking people's legs and feet. Once I remember him taking some vines with nettles on them from a tree and whipping me. I tried to joke it off, but it stung. He had long blonde hair down to his waist, often wore a white cap, and I doubt he showered more than once a month. He was very proud of his father and of being a Chase. He knew the way they lived was strange and it made him feel important. One day I was talking about movies I'd seen and he said, "I've got more important things to do than waste two hours of my time watching a movie." Kate mocked him on my behalf, but Barca made himself clear.

Not surprisingly, Barca had a hard time fitting in at school. On appearance alone he stood out loudly. His wild-boy nature must've shocked his teachers and peers. He didn't have any friends there and he didn't want to go to school anymore. Barca thought he was smart enough already and all he needed to know he would learn from his family better than he would at any school. Barca was only in the fourth grade, but his brothers were mostly in their mid to late twenties and still lived on the farm, so he figured he'd obviously be able to function without a diploma. Quill and Mal argued that, living as a Chase, it was important to develop social skills outside of the family, to see how other Americans lived. It was difficult to get perspective on the inside. Quill felt that social skills were what he got out of the Paso Robles school system, and he was a friendly and beautiful man, never making you feel inferior in any way, but treating everyone as an equal. Barca was obstinate, though, and was too alienated to see why he should ever have to go to that "stupid school" again.

"Hal's genius is years beyond yours or mine," Casey wrote me once, and I agreed. There sat Hal at the head of the table, where he always sat, a smiling St. Nick. As a gift to the natives, Casey brought an old-fashioned maze game to the family, one where you balanced the board with your hand and guided a small silver pinball through the track, avoiding the black hole pitfalls that sucked up the ball and made you start from the beginning. There were a number of these holes, and finishing the course was an accomplishment for me, but Hal sat and fiddled with the game for hours. So did

Barca and Tubloq. In fact, Barca got very good at it.

One day Hal told me that the day before he had tested himself to see what ratio of beer to coffee made him play the best. One Blatz beer to two cups of coffee, or three cups of coffee to one Blatz, or three Blatz's to four cups of coffee, or five cups of coffee to two Blatz's? The possibilities were endless and he was really curious under what conditions his mind and body could control this pinball, because… Because I don't know why. Was he comparing results at his age? Was he gauging the mental state he wanted to be under all the time? Or was he bored?

Hal admitted boredom was a constant topic of his youth. Jack Kerouac confessed to

Hal that much of his art was completed out of boredom, or that boredom caused the completion of his writing, and Hal said that William S. Burroughs was the most bored person he'd ever met.

Basically he was telling us that the most exciting literary movement to come out of the second half of the American 20th century was born out of boredom (not to say it isn't so in all centuries too). Casey was endlessly intrigued by this. I remember him gazing at Hal with those devious eyes of his, interested and gleaming, looking amazed at the slightest word, thought, or image. Casey couldn't get over what Hal was saying because X, Casey's avatar, was the most bored person Casey ever met, bored as only a genius can be. So bored he lived on a "liquid diet" and after being diagnosed with cancer shot himself in the head on Mt. Tam.

"I can barely drink coffee let alone live on a liquid diet so I can never know what X was thinking," said Casey, "and how can I write an internal monologue for a character if I don't know what he's thinking?"

It was an incredible point that afternoon, art stemmed from boredom. It was one of those reversals of all logic like depression equaling humor. Who's to say that when Hal fiddled with the $1 maze game (perfect for Hal too, so 1930s – a game impossible to imagine a modern-day man having any fun with at all, no batteries or electricity, just wood and a ball), it wasn't a byproduct of the old man's boredom?

Hal created a test and experiment for himself in drug use with caffeine and beer as the sample drugs. It was another afternoon, the sun was shining out the window, Kate was baking bread, Martha was bent over the stove, Barca was saying something he wasn't listening to, and Hal was bored. He wouldn't admit it but maybe he was. Hal would probably make up some very pragmatic reason for doing his tests with the game like he wanted to see the state of inebriation his reflexes worked best at for the making of his medieval instruments (which he worked on every day). If Hal knew this he could increase his efficiency, so it only stood to reason, right?

    Living in Quill's cabin I was high not only on marijuana but the idea that I was helping

Casey write a classic book on a forgotten genius of the '60s. I couldn't believe I'd been appointed. The days Casey wasn't too depressed to talk, I had visions of myself being a young Samuel Beckett, reading to James Joyce his masterpiece *Finnegan's Wake*. A strange hallucination, considering Casey could see (Joyce was blind), but when he was lying in Quill's bed downstairs in the late afternoon, smoke covering the sky, sunset a flaming orange like the color in Chinese paintings, the covers pulled over his sick, unwashed body (sick from love and sexual longing), I could swear he was going to die. I'd be the last person to see Casey alive, reading to him his final, most important work, his unfinished masterpiece.

I couldn't foresee I'd try writing this book five years ago when I was at Hal's. At the time, I was only interested in learning from the man. I didn't have dreams like Casey and Roger did. Roger Wing was the one who introduced us to the whole scene through Mark Wyatt, a Paso Robles native who went to high school with the Chases and whose dad, John, owned a nice spread of land himself off Highway 41, also know as the road where the end came for James Dean. It was vineyard land that John let go to waste through alcoholism and madness. He was a maverick physics professor at UC Berkeley in the '60s and from a family of physicists who worked at NASA to help launch the first astronauts into space. John wanted to live a Hal-like life on his land, but obviously lacked Hal's focus and depth. He listened to the radio, watched TV, ate dinner with his wife, and drank gallons of wine as his family unraveled around him. But he thought himself a poet-philosopher iconoclast who exiled himself from the world for his singular pursuits. For a brief time, he'd transformed the barn, Mark's workplace as a sculptor, into a laboratory. Roger Wing was friends with Mark Wyatt, a friend of mine too from Santa Cruz (Quill went to Santa Cruz for a couple of years, but didn't graduate). Roger had far flung visions of the two of them creating sculptures together in the hills of Paso Robles. The Wyatt's property was complete with a workspace and the Chases were nearby. Both were fresh from college, but Mark was recently divorced with children. They smoked a lot of weed and drove each other mad, but not without doing one memorable sculpture together, a huge wooden sphere of interlocking strands of wood called "The Orb." "Tentacles and Testicles," I called it, and everyone laughed.

Roger dreamt not only of sculptures in Paso Robles, but of Hal. Mark Wyatt introduced Roger to the family and from the word go he was lost in their drama. Before Casey and I were on the scene, Roger was blown away by this man who reminded him of a character in James Agee's book *Let Us Now Praise Famous Men*, about salt of the earth people from the '30s depression era Appalachian mountains. But Hal wasn't poor. Paso Robles land, like everything else in California, was expensive. Hal was also an intellectual but the wooden table and the kids in dirty white clothes, no TV or radio, everyone running around barefoot, Martha over the stove, Kate sleeping in a little bed with Barca, Tubloq sleeping on the roof with the pigeons (his favorite bird), was too much for the dreamer in Roger. The Chases were all so happy, healthy and strong, held up by Hal's idealism, that Roger really believed they were holding the whole State of California together. Plus he had it bad for one of Hal's daughters, milk/cheese Hester. Roger wanted in on the drama so bad he ostensibly moved in with Mark Wyatt down the road to make art, but that was only half the vision. The other half revolved around becoming Hal's son.

The first night I met Hal I had such a headache I couldn't see straight. Roger and Mark had taken me to the Chase home for dinner. When the meal was over the family dispersed from the table, and Roger turned to Hester with the long blonde hair, rustic smile, and clear blue eyes. He gave her his big aquamarine eyes and long lashes, and said, "Gee, Hester, can I help you milk the cows?" She said sure, but matter-of-factly, and Roger became an 1800's suitor right before my eyes. I couldn't get over how this man who could blow hundreds of dollars in a bar in a night had the temerity to ask Hester if he could help her milk the cows!

Of course, their romance went nowhere. Hester ended up with Enrique, a Mexican field worker, and Quill ended up with a country girl. It would be hard to imagine any Chase, save Hannah the intellectual, getting involved with anyone outside the life. It would be impossible to enter the fiction that way unless you were born into it, or made the similar transformations that Hal did by voluntarily becoming a peasant. The metamorphosis would have to be complete before you could enter the Chase family. Those kids weren't in for a college romance. They worked hard every day, believed in family, and their mate would have to live like them if they were to live with them at all. Roger wanted to make the transformation (become Hal) but he was only a seedling.

It was via Roger Wing that Casey and I entered the picture at all, and from Mark Wyatt with his odd, noble voice, floppy hesitations, and his sense of humor one beat behind the punch line. Mark lived under his parents' rule and would get so stoned sometimes, so mad in his mind, you wondered if he knew where he was. Mark looked to the Chases reverently, but was intimidated by Hal. He saw the Chases taking over Paso Robles one day when the old man drifted away, becoming spiritual kings of a town falling the way of Southern California.

As much as Mark Wyatt was loved by the Chase family, he couldn't get over feeling inferior in their company. They were so strong and sure of themselves that ambiguity in character could make anyone feel weak around them. Not that they tried to make you feel that way. Actually, the Chases were open, warm, and usually gave you friendly smiles when you walked in, but Hal had reality "by the balls" (Casey's words), and anyone that strong scares the weak. The mirror of Chase life could warp a visitor's mind and make you wonder if you were alive at all.

Once Hal told me everyone in society was a slave and I pointed to Hester moving in the background and said, "You're a slave to Hester, Hal." He emphatically said, "You're right, I am." Hester said nothing.

By the end of my three-week stay I felt as physically and mentally strong as I've felt in my life. I could create my own reality. Spending time with Hal was like playing a game of chess that never ended, and the more I played, the stronger my mind became. When I looked at his reality, and looked at Casey's, I couldn't help but think the old man was right, and art was madness. It had obviously ruined Casey, it ruined Hal's Beat friends, and it would ruin me.

I was only barely starting my life as a writer at 25, and it was easy to see spraying out in many directions at once. I had committed to art by that age, but our marriage hadn't been a long one yet, and I could still see myself above it all. I could be Hal and an artist at the same time, a mixture of the geniuses to the left and right of me. If I could play chess with the master, or even have him entertain playing chess with me, I could be a master, looking at the middle road of life, with all the compassion and wisdom in my heart. I could go up in a personality blaze but see myself through the smoke and make art out of my life because I was stronger than the average man. I was Raskolnikov, by virtue of Hal, certain I was one of the exceptional people if only because I was in Hal's company, graced by his mind.

Hal was so intelligent when he talked about banking, money and world trends. He had a complete look of knowing in his eye after rattling off various details about how the world was run and would be run in the future. I'd ask Hal to repeat himself and he would, then I'd ask the best questions I knew how on the nature of society. Generally, Casey wouldn't participate in these conversations. He was more interested in the emotional nature of the man. Hal would answer my questions thoughtfully, and when I didn't understand I often pretended I did, thinking I could trace back his answer later. As a child, I enjoyed tracing how conversations started one place and ended up another. Once I told Hal that when I was a kid I used to read words backwards all the time to see how they looked and sounded. He said, "That's good," and showed me a piece of paper with letters jumbled all over them, and rearranged words.

When the old man talked his sentences were long and complicated, theoretical for a man of the soil. Hal really felt the abstraction of modern man. When I saw that his life was built from his books and that he'd spent years in the library as an undergraduate and graduate student at Columbia University, studying Native American ethnographies, Hal's vision made sense. He told me anthropology was nothing but the study of cultural relativism. That was the main point to be understood – cultural relativism. Hal studied ethnographies of Indian and Mexican cultures, obviously comparing them to his own, and became so repulsed by the U.S. he decided to live outside of it while still in it. Hal took to building boats like Noah preparing for the floods. When I was there a massive boat was nearly finished. It sat by the nuthouse where they kept the almonds, a short uphill walk through shrubs and leaves from Quill's cabin where Casey and I were staying. It was Quill's project but the family all had their fingers in the pie. If Hal could do it with his mind, so could I. I could do nothing or I could do anything, and Hal made me feel like I could do everything, so when I left Paso Robles I'd become more vital than I'd ever been before. Every reality was relative to the culture it came from, and I could make my own reality, based on my theories of relativity. Just as Hal had studied other cultures, I was studying Hal. We all did. Anyone who ecnountered him couldn't help but wonder how he was living this way in America in 1993.

"Bobby Kennedy was the last chance this Country had," Hal told me once. "He went into the Kentucky coal mines and went out and tried to really reach the people. No one has done that since. Certainly, his brother the president never did it. Bobby Kennedy was on the verge of leading America in a new direction. Now society wants to take everything from you; they don't want you to feel."

I remember Hal standing as he spoke, walking off his thoughts. I'm sure that Hal, as a young man, walked endlessly, but in old age he spent much of the day in his chair. Still, I could see the youth in him taking a walk and saying what he felt, what he believed, and what he wanted from life. Now he was living that vision free from the prison he saw society as, but not free enough to cause him endless worry and concern. He saw the beast from the south encroaching.

    Hal felt he had to fight with all the power in his mind to secure his land and family. Like an Indian in the old west fearing the white man, seeing him, or thinking he saw him. But Hal was the white man, and the tables had turned. His son, Tubloq, carried an Indian name, and there sat Hal in his chair with his moccasins, a can of beer, and his one off-white shirt seeing the evil out of the corner of his eye come to destroy nature and conquer the land. Hal and his family would fight until they were too overcome by numbers, then they'd flee in their boats, beating an exit to the coast 30 miles away, choosing and plotting a route years beforehand that would protect them well against ambush. Once to the sea, the family would understand, and be more than competent in the jobs they were given. Kate would man the wheel, Mal the sails and the dirty work, Quill would run around the ship fixing everything that needed fixing while navigating, and Martha would be in the galley peeling onions. They'd have a number of days they'd plan to be out at sea, and their rations and endurance would be gauged by that. When they got to land, the Chases would befriend the natives with goodwill. They'd have no objection to living off the land, and sharing resources with the people they met, assuming they were willing to do the same. Money would be obliterated. Hal and the kids would trade with the natives, choosing a barter economy based on function and necessity.

The cowboys could have their land and smoke all the tobacco they wanted. Hal and his tribe would escape the arrows of destiny and land free, but they'd have to be driven off first. Hal chose to make his stand in Paso Robles where the air was good and his children were healthy. The family's escape plan would be foolproof, because every great society not only planned for its rise but also its fall, but it was going to take more than idle threats from the town to kick Hal off. He'd sat there for 10 years, and he'd sit for another 10 too, one wife by his side, one in waiting, until the white man came.

In my youthful gaze Hal must have seen reflections of his passions before they turned to family, and he was able to play a song he loved to me and Casey, but on an instrument kept in the closet for so long he was impressed it still blew. That's how I thought of Hal's voice and his thoughts that summer. His ideas and intellect had the feeling of a swelling composition to them, oddly his own. I know that Hal, like a great musician, was proud to play again and not only to see he could do it but that I could hear one of his voices coming out. Hal was an instrument I haven't heard before or since, and it was easy to get lost in the murmur of his thoughts. "Martha, get me some more coffee." She put some grounds into a pot of boiling water. "Is there any more beer? Do you want some beer, Seth?"

"I'm fine."

"Maybe a beer and a cup of coffee for me," Hal said, sinking the ball unsuccessfully into the hole of the maze game. "Yesterday I had two cups of coffee and one beer, and I made it through this maze five times in a row. I'll bet at one cup of coffee and one beer I'll make it through at least five times."

I smiled and Hal smiled back, turning to face me with the game in his hands. He opened his can of beer and took a sip.

"How about if I drink the beer faster than I drink the coffee. Think I'll make it through at least five times still?"

"Sure."

"No way," said Barca, head barely above the table, bouncing up and down. "Gimme the game, Dad." Hal gave it up and waited for his cup of cowboy coffee.

Casey was playing the piano in the other room, talking to Hannah.

"Sounds like a cocktail lounge," Hal said of Casey's piano, and he guffawed, raising his arms from the table and waltzing them in the air as a mock piano player would. "In the '40's you used to hear this everywhere you went in New York. Where's the cocktails, Martha?"

She smiled and poured him his coffee from the pot.

Casey walked in from the other room wearing a Chicago Bulls T-shirt.

"Why do you wear that?" Hal asked seriously, remembering the days he was in society and everyone wore white, gray, or plaid.

"Thanks for the hello," said Casey. "But, since you ask, someone gave it to me for free."

"You're advertising the Bulls. You're not living for yourself, Casey. You're living through Michael Jordan."

Casey shook his head and smiled, speechless.

"Everyone wears these in society," I threw in. "Everyone in L.A. wears shirts advertising something else or someone else, Hal, and they don't think twice about it, not even once about it. It's just a shirt."

"Just a shirt?"

"It's what people wear."

Hal was incredulous. He knitted his brows and looked through us. Kate placed some bread on the table, fresh from the oven.

"You know what you're saying? You're saying everyone's a slave, Seth. Has business got it down so pat they don't even have to pay for their advertising anymore? They actually get you to pay for it! You're a poet, Casey, how can't you think what you're doing when you wear that shirt?"

"I didn't pay for it, Hal, and everyone wears these. They are every day."

Hal finished his first cup of cowboy coffee and first beer and was playing the handheld wooden game to see how many times he could go through the maze without sinking the miniature pinball in a hole. From that day on, Casey and I wore only solid-colored T-shirts to the dinner table, for Hal's sake.

One afternoon when I was alone with the old man and a couple of the kids he brought up Casey's book. "You do realize it might be published one day. Have you ever thought of what you're going to do then?"

"Not really, Hal. To be honest, I can't imagine the book ending. It's 1000 interchangeable pages long. You can read it in any order."

Hal took his fish eye off me and back to the table, scattered with books and plates. "Does Casey know why he's writing the book?"

"I'm not sure, Hal. He wanted to remember his best friend, his guru, the person who changed him most in his life."

"I think Casey hates X for dying," Hal added quickly. "He's mad at him for leaving him alone, and drinking himself to death, but Casey doesn't know it."

"I don't know what Casey thinks. He says he's got to go through his depression right now to get closer to where X was coming from, so he can write about him. The problem is Casey is not drunk, he's just depressed. I don't know what to say about the book, Hal. It's more a description of an internalized headspace than anything else. There's not much description of Marin, or the way anything looked. Not like when Thomas Wolfe wrote about the wind ripping through him on a New York City street, and how all the windows looked on the street."

Hal had a gleam in his eye. "How did Thomas Wolfe feel that much? Incredible, isn't it?"

"You should see Casey's painting at the nuthouse," chirped in Barca. "It shows him and his kids, but it's scary."

"That's all right," said Hal, "that's what he has to be painting now." Barca sat looking ahead. "And he's mad at his friend, that's why he's writing this book."

"Do you think, Hal?"

"Of course, I do. Why else would he be so obsessed thinking about him?"

"Much of the tone is angry," I concurred. "You know, Casey wrote a eulogy for X's wake and it was called *His Jokes are Funny, Not Yours.*"

"I know," said Hal, "it's painful remembering." A moment later he added:

"Casey needs to sell his paintings. I told him he should go to New York and walk up and down the streets from gallery to gallery. That's what painters do there."

"But Hal, Casey is 60 years old, and he's barely sold anything in his life. Do you really see that happening? He doesn't believe in selling paintings."

"Hal knows what we're thinking even when we don't know what we're thinking," said Casey. "He used X's line 'You don't want to know' at the end of the subject on Kerouac. That's just what X told me, 'You don't want to know, Case, because you are too much of a headcase.' But I'm thinkin' you don't want me to know how square you really are? But I don't know if that's what Hal is thinkin'. Like when he got us in denial about being Jewish. I said to him, 'Seth and I are coming from an enlightened head space, we're not trying to identify ourselves,' but Hal wouldn't buy that. No, sir. He was right, and he was going to tell us how he was right, but Goddamn him! We are sick of being Jewish!

"I never thought this was going to happen to me. Do you think when I was a young dude gettin' laid I thought one day I was going to be the living incarnation of my mother? Fuck no! Johnny is laughing at me about it right now, he'd Jew-bait me all night long. With Hal I was in denial about being Jewish, but with Johnny I was a middle-class Jew and that's all I'd ever be. 'You are what you hate,' he'd say.

"Did I bait X about coming from a white trash family and being the Okie spy? He was allowed to be whatever he wanted to be, an aristocratic bum, an itinerant musician, but I was a middle-class Jew. You know I have no money, I'd tell him let it rest, but he couldn't. Johnny would blow his cigarette smoke in my face in my pad, smoke all my dope, and tell me how middle-class square I really was. It made no sense. His friends were all Jewish. How deep is the shallow end?!?"

Casey paced Quill's cabin after talking, hunched over a table packing bowls of weed, and then lay on his bunk in the shade of the afternoon. He'd talk and I'd read his manuscript to him. He liked the way I read. We'd decide if the page made any sense in relation to X or if it was rambling on, psychobabble style. It became evident, however, no matter how clear or garbled certain pages were, the book hadn't written itself. Hal said it: "Casey has to write it, Seth, not you." I wholeheartedly agreed. How could I write a book on a man I didn't know, a group of friends I never had, or a town I didn't live in? But in my mind that was the test.

If Casey had been a good enough storyteller through his art that included not only the X manuscript but tons of photos of John Stephens because Casey was convinced part of the reason X befriended him was he wanted someone to photo document his life. And if John Stephens had been a thorough enough documentarian by letting slip to Casey *The Vagrant's Handbook,* a live cassette of the musical comedy the *Dope Operetta* starring Heavy Early, little notepads of doodles, lists, poems, scattered writings of a character named Bob, cassettes of X playing guitar and singing '40s standards like *All the Sad Young Men*. Well, I should have had a good enough feel to write about someone I only knew through art.

We didn't do the "once more without feeling" test even though Hal said X was a fictional character and we talked about him as an invention. I didn't think I could write a funny enough joke about a genius of a generation without talking to him first, or being stung by him at least once. It was too impossible to describe the '60s if you weren't there. Casey was using me as a guinea pig to see if he could make sense of X to someone who wasn't there. If it didn't work on me, it wouldn't work on anyone.

Hal's children lived their life in Paso Robles and probably would never leave the September winds that blew hot through an Indian summer or the oak meadows that undulated like the sea. Hal and Martha didn't constantly bicker over the little things, but looked to the bigger things by taking care of the little things everyday, and by taking care of each other, loving each other, and tying knots around the haloes in each other's eyes. I can't imagine Hal's children being ashamed or embarrassed for the life they lead (as I am). Their life was given to them by a higher hand, Hal's hand, and their place in his world was guaranteed at birth.

Each, of course, had a unique position on the farm. Hal was no stupid general. He knew certain men had abilities and talents others simply didn't, and I wish I'd asked him to explain his theory for this. As for Hal's daughters, their purpose was clear. Because they were women they attended to women's work like cooking, cleaning and taking care of the old man in his chair. All of the women and all of the men could perform any task on the farm if the moment needed them. In fact, they could perform multiple tasks at once, any of which was beyond my reach. I felt like a mouse in comparison to the Chases when Hester taught me the correct way to hammer in a nail.

    I remember Quill standing in the garden outside his cabin, tending to the irrigation system he built, and looking to the trees that blurred in the distance. He told me the world was an incredible place in which to be alive, a daydream really, but in the same breath wondered if maybe his life was too much of a daydream. Not that Quill didn't work hard for who he was; he worked harder than most men, but the work was under the sun with the family he loved. The work was what rooted him to the land, what watered him and bent him as he grew towards the sun, as it did for the entire family. But somewhere in his heart was the thought maybe life wasn't supposed to be so grounded and rooted, maybe you were meant to be yanked by the roots and exposed to the machinery of civilization: the city traffic, police whistles, and women with babies in their arms, faces smudged, standing on freeway ramps begging for change.

It was a struggle Quill knew his father went through, from Columbia to professor to peasant. Hal fought daily against the madness in New York City and the U.S.

The U.S. said: "Hal, if you think you got the mind and the strength to do it, go ahead and build your boats, houses, and families... Go write the book of your life... Go native," and Hal listened. He broke free, because the TVs, radios, jobs, toilets and trash men were all byproducts of an addiction Hal had a taste of but wanted no more.

He said, "I'll escape through my family," and he did. But the kids didn't have to go through the struggle to kick the addiction like the old man did. They were spared from getting down on their knees and begging, "Enough is enough. I've had it with this country's shit, I want out!" They didn't know the struggles of luxury: clean, ironed clothes, telephones to answer, TVs you had to fight to turn off, taxi rides you had to tip on, and conversations you faked. Hal gave his children work all right, but he didn't give them the feeling of being a prisoner with a ball and a chain tied around their ankles, running through the woods, past the freeways and mini-malls of America, past parking lots of onlookers shopping with their children, all life sucked from their faces. Hal stood up and cut the umbilical cord with his teeth for everyone.

It took more than thinking of knives, forks and office hours to do it. Hal gave his children thought, action and will. Quill knew it when he was staring at the trees from his garden that day, like a tree himself, wondering if there could be more to life. Was escape from Paso Robles possible? Where would the wind, trees and sky feel better?

Hal told a story to Casey once about how Allen Ginsberg was always travelling around, telling him about the beautiful places and people he'd seen in the world, all the cultures and non-cultures he'd visited. Hal said: "That's the difference between you and me, Allen. You keep finding paradise and leaving it. When I found it I stayed."

"I wanted what Hal has," Casey confessed to me sitting in the cabin. "I wanted family; I was ready. I love my kids. But that bitch (Anne) fucked me up, man."

"It was a welfare family you had, Casey, not a family like Hal's."

"Look, to be an artist in America you have to choose not to survive. I've told you that. It's the weirdest thing, but the minute you survive or make anything of yourself you're fucked. You'll never make anything good again. You'll be a so-and-so kinda writer, and the minute you try to do something different no one will take you seriously ever."

"So how do you live?"

"I told ya. If you're an artist in America you don't exist, period. You don't think about work, talk about work, look for work – you don't exist!"

"He's a child," I could hear Hal whisper in my mind. "Casey doesn't think he has to work. He either lives off other people or the State, that's all." But I said nothing.

"Why can't you be a non-famous painter who occasionally sells a painting, Casey?" I asked instead.

"I'm not going to swim in those circles, man. Show up on time? Forget it. I'll say what I want wherever I want. I already have the freedom to make bad art, why do I need to deal with that shit?"

"Money?"

"Art and money don't mix. Hal knows that. Why is he telling me to sell my paintings in New York City?"

"He wants you to survive, Casey."

Casey looked down at Quill's wooden table, no dentures in his mouth, only gums, and there was a silence.

"I can't even count past 500, man. What do I know about making money?"

Casey stopped to light a bowl of weed, stood up, and paced the hot wooden cabin. We had no choice but to stay inside where there were shadows, a ceiling, and one could try to forget himself. I read to Casey a long Marcel Duchamp interview. Casey was terrified and blown away by Duchamp's mind, which expounded upon how painting had reached its apex and was now officially dead.

"Bad news for painters," Casey said. We also read a Playboy interview with Charles

Bukowski where he confessed he didn't get laid until he was 24, and that he enjoyed masturbating more than real sex, it took more imagination. More often than not, however, we said nothing to each other at all.

    Casey really just wanted to get laid so he could forget about his break-up with Anne. Being 60 years old, and put up by Hal with no room anywhere in California to really call his own, he was desperate. The relationship with Hal living-wise was tenuous too. We were there to work on the book (WORK, WORK, WORK). As long as we were working Hal respected us, and never even asked Casey to let him read the manuscript. But work on *X* hit a brick wall and, to compound the problem, Casey and Hannah were attracted to each other"I do things to be a fictional character," Casey admitted to me once. "I travelled to Mexico to watch an eclipse. I travelled around the U.S. in a Ford Cobra that belonged to the Kingston Trio's lead singer." Casey had it all written in a poem called NOW... Now I'm in Japan playing drums...Now I'm on a mountain in India.... ad infinitum. Now Casey was on Hal's farm, as great as any fiction. Being the actor/storyteller he was, Casey dropped himself right into the drama. It wasn't enough to meet Beat legend farmer Hal Chase, the man who introduced Jack Kerouac to Neal Cassady and who now lived like a Jeffersonian idealist in a land all his own, ethnographies swirling in his head. Casey had to have one of the girls, too.

He had to kick his heels into the text, dance a little, and shake things up on the inside. Every great story has a doomed love in it somewhere, and that Casey's doom would mix him up with Hal was inevitable. They were like two stars flying in space, one stronger than other, but two stars nevertheless, whose meeting alone was a direct hit. I was like some stardust on the outside twinkling in from another galaxy, riding the coattails of my own relationship explosion, but I was flying in too, and my life was also falling apart.

Casey wanted to fly into the pages of the book on Hal's life. I see it now, the imaginary novel, opened outside in the sun, near the shade of an oak tree, and surrounded by gold and green, its pages flapping in the wind, right outside the rickety structure of the house.

"Once I was playin' the harpsichord off the kitchen," Casey wrote, "heard but not seen

– and in Hannah comes, and while I keep playin' she hugs my head to her breast and whispers her love. I was so cool – acted like nothin's happenin' – kept playin' Bach-like runs – tellin' her not to think about the monkeys. I want her but it's impossible. She's too brilliant, strong, beautiful and young for me (she said I was too young for her!). She intimidates me with her beauty and told me that's how it is for her, very lonely."

I'd left Paso Robles by the time Casey and Hannah were snuffed out by Hal. All Casey had to do was show Hannah a poem of an imaginary meeting between Gertrude Stein and Albert Einstein (arroz is arroz is arroz, X punned) or show her the philosophy of John Brockman, the book where Casey taped the phrase "You'll never be the same after reading this" on the cover, and Hannah was gone. Hal told Casey he didn't think he was a "suitable suitor."

Most nights, Hannah would sit at the kitchen table, look unhappy, and say nothing. She had long brown hair, blue eyes, and a soft pudgy face. Since Hannah had yet to live off the farm, no amount of words could make up for her lack of worldly experience. She looked a peasant less than her brothers and sisters, but was still country to the bone. How could she want to be a writer in Hal's shadow? He was like a bust of knowledge sitting there at the head of the table, and she was one of his nine children, nothing more or less. Hannah didn't want to stay on the farm with the family, and nothing agitated Hal more. It was family or nothing on the inside. "I can't get over it," Hal said one night to Casey, ignoring Hannah and me as we ate."These two have never read Goethe. Two literary young people. How is that possible?"

I doubt Hannah could leave, none of them could, probably not even the one who left. Casey and college were illusions on the farm.

City life was an hallucination Hal did away with because the correct title of Jack Kerouac's first novel was *The Town and the Country*, not *The Town and the City,* right? Hal's life was little different than a man's a hundred years ago before the fears of population explosion, nuclear war, cloning, and global warming had disturbed mankind's sleep. Hal was turning back that little clock by his head while living in the present. It was 1993 but Hal and his kin dressed in dirty white shirts and work pants they wore seven days a week. It wasn't because they were migrant farmers from Mexico looking for sub-minimum wage work. It was because their father, Hal Chase, had made a conscious decision.

"Maybe someday someone will write a poem about me but I'm not holding my breath," he once said.

The artist in the modern world didn't disgust Hal, but he didn't understand how one could go on living until old age when all he did was create a cult of personality for art's sake, because Hal didn't think myopically. He saw life expanding before him not only in himself but also in his name, which he'd given to a robust family of nine to carry on in the noblest tradition, preparing for the winter in spring, and the spring in winter.

Every season had its meaning to man, every turn of the wheel, but unlike Hal I didn't plan well for the future. Good or bad I was trying to be an artist and lived like one with little future in mind, a hazy disposition that sucked me up into the dramas of my age. Hal must've felt this way at Columbia University once too. Despite his doom-saying, there existed deep in his character an optimism for the human race I can't fathom. To produce that many children would seem to say Hal believed the race should go on and could go on. I can't believe there wasn't a deep feeling in him that his family was to be a symbol for others to see, even if they were only a few, to contemplate as a protest against the modern world the U.S. had created. A protest lived in the fullest affirmation of life.

September was a month of longing and regret when an American kid went back to school to learn his ABCs, make friends, see old friends, and dream of love. A time when the world is most alive with expectation, and there is no drought of feeling. The light blazes an opaque blue, summer is over, and there is a certain white tint on the outlines of trees, cars and people that the harsher greens and yellows of summer omit. The fall light cuts, and September is the beginning of the change, because the world is ready to begin again.

Hal Chase was a famous literary figure, the only one I've ever met. Casey and I could live one book and make another. Feed and be fed by the Chases, until we exploded into reams of poetry. Hal Chase fueled the book on X, but he also overwhelmed it, because the book on Hal, yet to be written at the time, was monumental fiction itself.

Every time you entered his shack, or walked down the oak tree path to dinner, kids swinging on a rope over a creek that trickled by the cows, everyone dressed like a smiling peasant, you felt like you were in a book. I became a character in a book working on a book, who I always thought I was anyway. And Casey felt the same thing too. Under the blue skies of Paso Robles, we were flipping through an unforgettable chapter of our life, living fiction while making it. Hal was the oracle we questioned, glued to his chair at the head of the table, eyes drilling through us, cold blue and luminescent.

"What are you going to do if this book gets published? Have you thought of that?" he asked.

I had no answer. I was too immersed in the life I was living on Hal's farm to think of anything else. When Tubloq called me an honorary member of the family I wore it as a badge of honor. How could I imagine the implications of one book while living another? I was living in a world of consequence then, and felt everything I'd previously done had lead me to this place in Hal Chase's life. There was no going back.

But I went back. The morning I left for Santa Cruz I drove from Kiler Canyon road to Hal's for breakfast, something Casey and I rarely did. I ate franks and beans and hung out with Hal and Martha alone for a couple of hours. He built an angel's harp that stood right next to the table, a rare place for it, and Martha closed her eyes to play me a song. Of course, Hal didn't play the harp, he never played any of his instruments, and he just sat listening to her play, a smile on his lips. Martha apologized to me when she was done, she didn't think she played very well, but it was a beautiful piece of music. I drank cup after cup of cowboy coffee that morning. When I said goodbye, Hal stood with his arm around his wife at the front door of their shack, light pouring through the trees, and invited me back any time. They waved and watched my car pull away.

    The first place I stopped was the AM/PM in Paso Robles for gas. I gawked at the magazine rack, the employees in their red polyester shirts, the shriveled up hot dogs and the neon nacho cheese. America seemed decades away from Peachy Canyon, yet it was just down the street. It was only 10 AM and I decided to drive up the coast like an unconscious truck driver. I stopped at a Big Sur beach at one in the afternoon. The mountains bulged from the cliffs, and the waves crashed down. I walked in the sand and looked at every rock and pebble along the way. When I made it to the ocean no one was there. The mossy mountains behind me made picturesque slopes, and the sun was golden. The wind and the sound of waves made music. It was great to see the ocean after a 100-degree Indian summer in the dry oak meadows. I only remember one day of gray in Paso Robles and one day of smoke in the sky that made the sun look like it was filtered through gauze. Other than that it had blazed all September.

Looking out at the ocean stretching into infinity, making an uneven line against the sky, horizontal but not quite, I did push-ups and sit-ups while gazing at the waves. I crossed my legs like a yogi and imagined how incredible it would be to see Jenny in a couple of hours, my other fiction. I still remember Jenny's smile dripping with excitement when I came back to Santa Cruz later that day. I dreamt we'd go camping, sleep under the stars, and how I was capable of living any way I wanted to now. I could blaze a path for us straight to the sun, free of all the bullshit I created. I thought I could live a new way that afternoon. Spirited by three weeks with Hal, I wouldn't be a slave to my fear anymore. I was no longer a puppet of my parents, hopelessly dangling on a string, weak in the face of nature. I'd just finished boot camp with two of the toughest generals and was now a man.

The morning I left Paso Robles, Casey thanked me for working on his book with him, though we never finished it. We were driving my car through the morning sun, dust flying up from the road, clouding the windshield. Looking straight ahead, Casey said it took courage to do what I did, to read 1000 pages of the Swami's. I agreed, though reading the manuscript didn't feel like the most courageous part of the adventure to me. I felt I could undertake any artistic process because my energy was great and I'd just had breakfast with Hal Chase.

Afterword

By

The Editorial Research Bureau

Like all poets and profligates, Seth Kupchick dreamt history would redeem him and that his unpublished works would be celebrated upon his death like John Kennedy Toole's *A Confederacy of Dunces* or Marina Keegan's *The Opposite of Loneliness.* It's hard to understand what drives writers like Kupchick because the chance of having their life's work absolved by history is rather far-fetched, especially if they haven't achieved any success in their lifetime, and by any barometer it is safe to say that Seth Kupchick lived his life in obscurity. He may have been one in a million, and the few who knew him may have been touched by the sheer bravado of his intellect or the depth of his humor. His final years were spent as a pizza delivery driver where few of his coworkers understood his humor, but in the scope of his life this is a tangent. He'll be remembered for a rather thin but potent novella – *If So Carried by the Wind* – that we've done our best to reconstruct from his notebooks, and given Kupchick's longhand this wasn't easy.

Kupchick saw himself as a story writer but he mostly wrote novellas, a form with which he was never comfortable, because they weren't very popular in his day, before the internet took over publishing, and yet he seems not to have been able to do much else. The novellas of his twenties, though ambitious, lacked readability, and literally challenged the reader (and Kupchick?) to understand what he had done. The first novella that Kupchick considered a breakthrough was called *The Adventures of George Stentenculus* and read like a kief inspired story that William S. Burroughs or Paul Bowles could have written. But Kupchick had none of their control of grammar, or education, and chose to use dash marks instead of sentences, thus alienating most of the reading public right off the bat.

Nothing in the early work intimated the greatness Kupchick was to achieve in *If So Carried by the Wind,* a slim book where he finally found a voice that would set him apart from his peers.

Most artistic careers that blossom seemingly overnight are hard to understand, and from a teleological perspective there was nothing to indicate that Kupchick would break free from the experimental literature that he banged out for years with almost no audience.

We don't really know what he thought of the early works, except that he loved them all when working on them, but that's common for writers, unable to distinguish the good from the bad. He'd share them with his friends and from all accounts took their reactions very personally. He would lose sleep if he thought a friend he respected didn't like what he wrote, and this must've been hard, since they rarely did. By all accounts, Kupchick was primed for success in his late twenties when he moved to

Seattle, but quickly found disappointment. Like all lost souls he was flung into the hands of fate, which, ironically, lead him away from a predictable mediocrity, at least for a summer. He met some kindred souls who inadvertently released a new voice in him, and let Kupchick write the only story he really had to (more on this later).

The editorial research bureau doesn't like to revel in clichés and knows the literary weight of being an author who has died young, or disappeared like Kupchick, but that's not why we're resurrecting him. We really think *If So Carried by the Wind* is worthy. If our publication of Kupchick's posthumous (?) work sends shivers down his spine and into the publishing world of New York City, then we apologize. As for authenticity, we're pretty sure the story is real but even that is up for debate. Nothing Kupchick wrote before this breakthrough was autobiographical, and many authors never make such a radical shift, but Kupchick is no regular author. It has been said that he was hoping his contribution to *X* would vault him to literary fame but as an editor, or a contributor on a project. "I'm not the integral factor," was one of Kupchick's favorite sayings in college, but how wrong he was and how ironic in his wrongness!

Kupchick treated the idea of being a writer ambiguously, like everything else in his life. His grammar was terrible, perhaps due to his experimental early education, and he didn't like reading much as a child, though we dug out of one of his notebooks that he learned to read at two. Kupchick preferred TV to literature for most of his life but joined the "kill your television" movement when he went to U.C. Santa Cruz for a leftist education and was taught that advertising, his father's profession, was responsible for brainwashing the masses into mindless consumerism. He did well in school but was never the best, and the summer after freshman year decided to educate himself, believing that college had taken him away from being a scholar.

He got a job in a shoe warehouse, like the narrator of Tennessee Williams's *The Glass Menagerie*, and would eat turkey sandwiches on his lunch break on the sidewalk like a working-class grunt, albeit with bougainvillea in the background. Kupchick would come home to his teenage room, get high, and read Kesey, Steinbeck or Huxley. He wanted to get his "cinematic ideas" out into the world through writing, and imagining art through a personal lens.

Reconstructing *If So Carried by the Wind* has not been an easy task. The editors have come to believe that Kupchick's artistic vision was to create one seamless notebook. He'd read Genet's *Our Lady of the Flowers* and the way that novel segued from a fantasy to a prison autobiography was so lucid to Kupchick, he wanted to recreate it in his notebooks. It's almost like he hoped that a journal entry and an attempt at fiction could be read back to back and make a poem, but we must remember

Kupchick was in his twenties and must've believed in the freedom of an ever-expansive art.

The notebooks have little bits of every part of Kupchick's life from bills to letters written to his parents he never sent, but he made attempts at organization by numbering the stories. He also drew in the notebooks and painted much during this time, which must've made him think that the notebooks in their pure state were his art and, if Kupchick's storage space is any proof, they take up a lot of ground. It's easy to imagine that, in his grab for immortality, Kupchick envisioned the notebooks being preserved in the Smithsonian, or sold at art auctions for thousands. Especially the longhand of *If So Carried by the Wind*.

If So Carried by the Wind is really two stories, because Kupchick wrote one about his actual life, a new thing for him, called *The Mad Captain*. In the summer of '98, Kupchick and his longtime girlfriend, who handed over the notebooks, were moving out of their first apartment, and he moved into a house with a complex drunken wannabe rock star, the Mad Captain, a man who took Kupchick out of his shell and gave him a moment's breath to let out his life's work, but unfortunately Kupchick has disappeared. We don't think he will ever truly disappear, since we've taken it upon ourselves to manicure and publish this unusually brilliant document.

The summer of 1998 was a good season for Kupchick's creativity. It may have been the last time he was so creative, but recreating a scene like 4309, the house that fate threw him into, was impossible. It was Dada without trying to be, and by all accounts he and his roommates would have jam sessions all night, or until the Mad Captain passed out with his legs crossed and a cigarette in his hand. We don't know how but where Kupchick wrote *If So Carried by the Wind,* and one could suspect at least two or three sessions were done in the dead of night, or the early morning light, with a drunken grin. Thankfully, we know when Kupchick wrote them because he'd date his notebooks to arrange the seamless work he dreamt of, but he didn't do much more.

We have come to the conclusion that *If So Carried by The Wind* should be read in its entirety. *The Mad Captain* is a worthy story and, if Kupchick had written more short stories, it would be a star in the collection. We thought of weaving it into the main story, and we're sure nothing would've made Kupchick happier because it's just perverse enough to alienate even the hint of an audience, but we're not that perverse.

The Mad Captain would seem to imply that Hal Chase, the protagonist of *If So Carried by The Wind,* had driven Kupchick into an artistic corner, where the only way out was to exhume him through fiction. The dream sequence was a piece we found in one of the many copies of the same story, with slight variations, that came down to us, and was a unique angle on the work, before Kupchick's disappearance.

Hal slept under the oaks with his family and the land was quiet save the rustling of critters in the hay and the smell of smoke from a fire. The creek murmured behind the house and it sang Hal to sleep, and his children slept in blankets under starlight. They went to bed early and rose early with their work being planned and prepared without question.

in the dream, the Mad Captain's duty was to himself and his songs.

"Where is this life leading you?" Hal asked him in the dream. They were on board an imaginary ship Hal built from scratch with

wood, nails and a hammer. A kerosene lamp sat on a desk and Hal ducked his head as he stood.

"All I know is I'm sick of everyone sleeping," answered the Mad Captain smiling while sitting in a chair cross-legged, taking a sip of Hal's wine. He wiped his lips with his sleeve and added, "'no fun' is not such an easy credo to live by when your family's not around, is it, ol' timer?"

"'No fun' constitutes life!" screamed Hal.

"You're going nowhere! You're the one who chose to self-destruct, not me. You're a slave to your personality!"

"You're a slave to an extension of your personality," the Mad Captain countered. "It's *called your family. Now c'mon, ol' man, have a drink, take a load off."*

"You're perpetuating your emotions for the sake of your art and it's perverse," Hal said in his high voice. "You're trapped inside your songs and don't even know it. You…"

The Mad Captain wasn't listening. He sat at the head of the table on a wooden chair and picked up a guitar off the wall and started playing.

"I too can see, just don't care, never wanted children mussin' up my hair." "You're a child!" screamed Hal as the Mad Captain played and sang. "You've still got a lunch box of Star Wars toys to prove it."

Soon Hal was back on the farm with his family and it was quiet as he awoke from sleep.

"Is everything fine?" he asked at the morning table, disturbed.

"Everything's fine," assured Kate. "Quill's working on the boat right now up at the nuthouse."

Hal stared at the table, only half soothed by his daughter's reply. Though he returned to the business of the day, he couldn't get the dream meeting with the Mad Captain out of his mind.

The Gen X novel is a lampoon of a novel and has no point of view (think of *Generation X* by Douglas Coupland, who single-handedly destroyed the novel, with catch words like

"McJob" taking the place of a plot). Kupchick's work is second rate at best but, unlike many of his peers, he fought for a voice and that's why we've chosen this work to be remembered, the only thing this unknown writer seemed to care about when he was alive (?) and still could've done something with his life. It's true that his rank as an author would be more impressive if this piece were longer, but it has one thing most novels twice the length don't, and that is when you get to the end you want it to go on, so it's not a failure. It's the voice that matters, the singularity of vision, the coming of age feeling he was able to express once in his life, before he happily disappeared, and could seemingly be remembered.

To give the author a respite, it's hard for most mortals to imagine what it would be like to write one immortal song, or poem, before you die, and how that would change you in ways the world would never know. It would seem that Kupchick didn't handle the feeling well, nor was he particularly lucky to strike a soaring success with this one novella, or what we like to call the great American mini-novel, but he deserved it. It's the voice of youth and you only have one chance to capture that.

Made in United States
Orlando, FL
05 June 2022